Raju's Ride

Story by Pratima Mitchell
Pictures by Stephen Waterhouse

OXFORD
UNIVERSITY PRESS

Raju and his baby sister were like the filling in a sandwich. Their parents took them to work with them every morning on a scooter.

PHUT-PHUT-PHUT!

2

When they got to their mango tree, Raju's mother and father got ready for the day's work and Raju went to school. The baby played on a blanket.

Raju went off to school with his bag on his back and a coin in his pocket. At break time he bought peanuts for himself and his friends.

All day long people brought their ironing to the mango tree. They brought sheets and shirts and saris. Raju's mother and father took turns to iron clothes all day long. The iron was very heavy. It made their backs very tired.

Parrots and squirrels and crows and doves loved the mango tree. They squawked and quarrelled. Sometimes they made a mess on the clothes. When Raju came back from school, he banged a drum to keep away the birds.

5

The children who lived in the big houses on the street didn't let Raju play with them.

"Go away! You're too young for our gang! Go and play with your baby sister!" they said.

Raju's mother said, "Never mind them Raju. You'll get big soon enough. Let's take the ironing back to Mrs Sen at Number 30."

They left the baby with Raju's father and walked to Number 30.

"Hello Raju," said Mrs Sen. "Done your homework? Here's a little treat for you."

She gave him three biscuits with pink icing on top. Raju smiled and said thank you.

When they got back to the mango tree, the monkey man was waiting in the shade.

"Look, Raju, look! Here are the lovely princess and the handsome prince!" he said.

The monkeys danced for Raju.

"They need a reward! What will you give them?"

Raju gave the boy monkey one biscuit. He gave
the girl monkey another biscuit. Raju's sister
started to cry, so he gave her the third pink biscuit.
   The big children were playing football in the
street. They shouted, "No, you can't play with us.
You're too young for our gang. Go and play with
your baby sister!"

"Wait till I finish these shirts Raju," his mother said. "Then we'll go to Number Five. Maybe the lady will have a treat for you."

Raju went with his mother to Number Five. The lady at Number Five gave him an orange. Raju put it down on the baby's blanket.

A cow came looking for something to eat. She saw the orange. But, before he could shoo her away, Raju's orange had gone into the cow's tummy.

The big children ran past rolling a hoop. Raju tried to run with them.

"No, you can't play with us. You're too young for our gang. Play with your baby sister!" they said.

"Don't worry about them Raju," said his father.
"Come, let's take these trousers back to Mr Nath."
    Mr Nath gave Raju three sweets – red, yellow
and green.

Raju left his sweets on the blanket next to the baby. All of a sudden, three fat doves flapped down from the mango tree. They each picked up a sweet and flew off. Raju threw sticks at the birds, but it was too late.

The big children were playing horses and carts. They galloped past Raju.

They cried, "You're too young for our gang! Play with your baby sister."

Raju's mother said, "Never mind Raju. Only one sheet left for Mrs Gupta. Let's take her back her ironing."

Mrs Gupta was having a tea party. She put a crisp, golden samosa in a paper bag for Raju.

On their way back to the mango tree, they stopped to say hello to Uncle Amir.

"What have you got there Raju?" asked Uncle Amir. "Yum-yum! I am so hungry."

Raju felt he had to give Uncle Amir a present. He gave him the crisp, golden samosa.

"Here's a present for you, Raju," Uncle Amir said, giving him a paper flag.

When they got back to the mango tree, Raju heard a very loud sound like a trumpet. Coming down the road was a huge grey elephant. The elephant swayed from side to side. Its legs were like tree trunks. Its feet were like rocks. It was as high as the mango tree.

The elephant stopped under the mango tree.
Down came its trunk and picked up the red flag.
He held it up in the air. Everyone clapped.

"That's not fair!" shouted Raju. "First I had three pink biscuits. Then I had an orange. Then I had three sweets. Then I had a samosa and then I had a flag. Now I haven't got anything!" He felt like crying.

19

"Would you like a ride on my elephant?" asked the elephant keeper.

"You take Raju home on your elephant and we'll follow you on the scooter," said Raju's father.

Raju couldn't believe his luck.

The elephant kneeled on its front legs. The keeper helped Raju to climb up into the seat. Then the elephant raised himself slowly on all four legs.

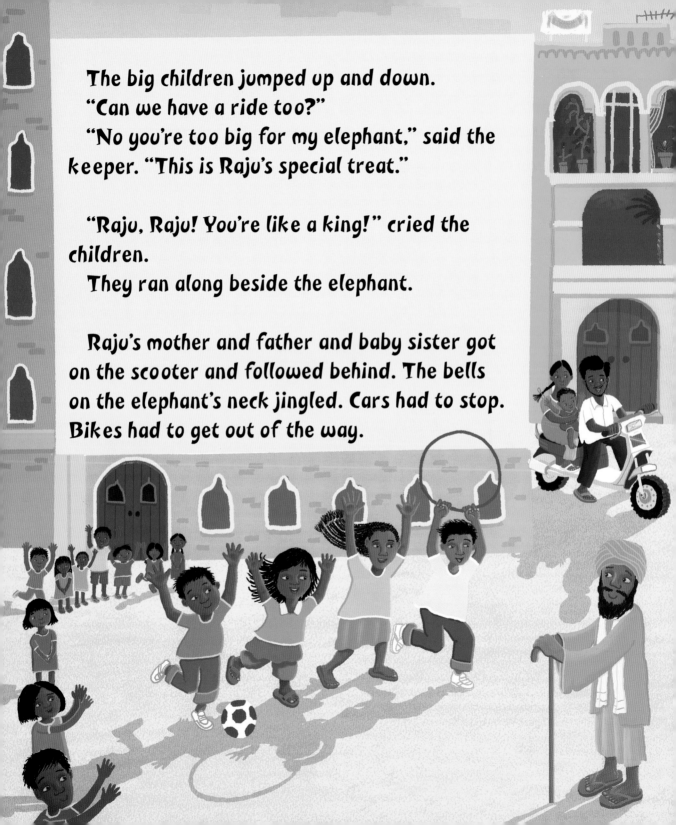

The big children jumped up and down.
"Can we have a ride too?"
"No you're too big for my elephant," said the keeper. "This is Raju's special treat."

"Raju, Raju! You're like a king!" cried the children.
They ran along beside the elephant.

Raju's mother and father and baby sister got on the scooter and followed behind. The bells on the elephant's neck jingled. Cars had to stop. Bikes had to get out of the way.

Raju waved at everyone. He touched the leaves on the trees. He felt like the most important person in the world.